GO WITH THE FLOW

Lily Williams &
Karen Schneemann

:01
First Second
New York

HAZELTON
HIGH SCHOOL
WELCOME
BACK,
STUDENTS!

Wakey, wakey, eggs... and *bakey!*
Who's ready for her first day of sophomore year?
YAWN
LA LA
LA LA LA

First stop: Christine's. **Second stop:** middle school. **Third stop:** high school. **Fourth stop:** work.

I wonder if Christine is awake.

Christine, up and at 'em!
KNOCK KNOCK

I'm on it.

Christine!
Brit is here!
NEW

BYYYYYYEEEEEEeeee!
NEWS

Are you serious, Christine?
We told Abby we'd meet her before first period.

BEEP
BEEP
BEEP
6:35
SNOOZE

Have a good day, Abs. Say hi to the girls for me.
SMOOCH
BEEP

THAT'S whyyy I WANT TO BE WITH youuuu! Oh Oh oh youuuu
SCROLL SCROLL

Sasha, it's your first day at a new school. Try to take your headphones off and make a friend.

Mm-hmm.

ZELTON
H SCHOOL

Good luck today, doofus!

RING
RI

NG
RING

RING RING

Cutting it close on the first day?

You can thank Christine.

I just really take this whole "beauty sleep" thing seriously. It is highly important to me to be the most stunning creature...

this school has ever seen.

Hmmm...

This is where you say, ***Oh, no, Christine, you can sleep less, you're already sheer perfection.***

Did you even brush your teeth this morning?

Pfsh.

Now I have to hike all the way to the 400s wing for APUSH.

Ah!
Okay!
I'm off to art.

BYYYEEE!

Is it just me...
or...
is this year going to *ROCK?!*

You always say that, and it never does.

This year it will.
I can feel it!

16-23-05

H2O POLO
wed
4pm
TRYOUTS
CROSS-
COUNTRY
tryouts!
4pm
golf

CROSS-COUNTRY
Tryouts!
JOIN US
TUESDAY @ 4PM

Sasha, an extracurricular activity would look good to colleges.
Maybe you'll meet a friend!

Tuesday, four p.m.

The usual route.

Down Lee Avenue and up the hill at the end, circle around the loop, and meet back here. I will be timing you.
Let's see what you've got.

SMACK

Chen.
You made JV.
See you tomorrow
at practice.

HHS JV
XCOUNTRY

So.

I heard you made JV.

Ha ha, yeah!

Maybe I can run with you guys at our run practices.

If you can keep up.

Okay!
Great!

See you at
RUN practice.

Does she know *anyone*
can make JV?

Don't mind Haven or Melly. Those girls are just—

Oh yeah, whatever.
I mean...

I don't need any charity friends.

No charity friend here.

I'm just the regular kind.

friday

Chip

Have you guys seen the new girl?
I think her name's Sophie...or maybe Tasha?

Huh?
You guys are taking English with Mrs. Malone, right? I heard her essay tests are really hard...
Maybe I should transfer into Mr. Chavez's class. But then that would mess up my math class and I would have to change from Mr. Plant to Mr. Ciao, and I love Mr. Plant, because of his themed Friday lessons. But I bet...
But then what if I fail and am forced to live as a sophomore ***FOREVER?!***

Then I guess you'll haunt the halls of Hazelton High School for ***ALL ETERNITY!***

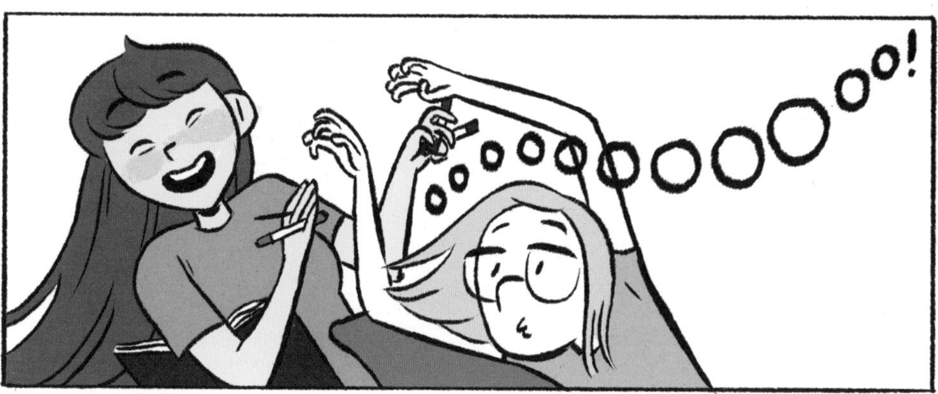
OOOOOOOOOOOOOOOO!

How on earth are you this riled up on the fifth day of school?

Oh, guys, quiet. Mr. Darcy is about to appear.

I bet.

Not a single dorknozzle that we go to school with will have turned into anything close to Mr. Darcy over the summer.

True.
But then who could ever compare to Mr. Darcy?

This is the part where he touches her hand.
sigh

Also,
I think we are reading *Jane Eyre* this year!

Isn't that the horror movie where the girl is locked in the attic?

That sounds terrifying.

It's a feminist romance story, Christine.

What are you working on, Abs?
Another masterpiece?

It's for an exhibit at the library.
They're putting on a show about feminist voices and activism.

So I'm just sketching some ideas.

Don't look at 'em yet!
I haven't figured it out.

All right, but you know I'm a serious art connoisseur.
Let me know if you need my insights.

CHOMP
CHOMP

I'll show you if I get chosen to be in it.

You'll get in. You're a feminist with a loud voice.

Brit...
throw me a cookie!

Okay, but seriously...

What English class are you guys in?

Wednesday,
September 4th

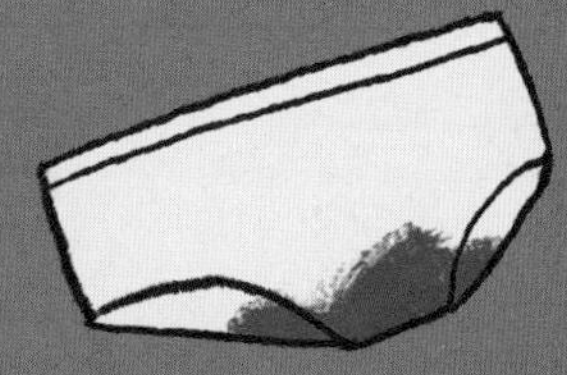

I LOVE YOU -DAD
3:30 TUES/T
CROSS-COUN
MOM PICK UP
TUES & DAD T

Hi! I'm Abby. Let's make our way to the bathroom.

Wh- what?

Howdy-do, Sasha. I'm Christine, and this is Brit.

We're on cross-country together.
Yeah... hi.

Why are we in the bathroom?

You got your period. And it's on your pants.

Oh no!
Oh no!
Oh nooo
no!

It's my
first one.
Go into the
stall. I'll get you
a pad from the
machine.

OH NO!
It's everywhere!

Don't worry! Spit on it nice and good...

and rub a little.

Ew.

Brit, that's not going to work. The machine is always empty.

EMPTY
SANITARY PADS

See, they never stock them. That's why I always carry an emergency pad. I don't even know why we have these machines.

It's so dumb. What if someone had an emergency, like Sasha?
Honestly, it's not even just that.
What if the machine was stocked but someone doesn't have the money? What if someone can't find a pad or tampon anywhere? Then what do they do?

I mean, it's fine.
I'm fine.
Here, put my sweatshirt around your waist.
It's not fine at all!

Duder, chill.
Injustices are everywhere, my friend.

Sanitary items are always an injustice. Did you know that most states tax them as "nonessential items"?

Abby gets very passionate about things.

Understatement.

Toilet paper is free in any public bathroom. So why aren't sanitary items?
People bleed! It is natural.

AND women already make less money than men and we get taxed higher on basic necessities. This seems criminal!

Whoa, I didn't know any of that.

It's the twenty-first century—how is this still happening?

A lot of people get their periods—it's not the end of the world. We'll help you through this.

But you don't get it. I have no friends. Like zero.
I'm so embarassed. Everyone saw!

I already look like I'm in junior high!
God, this is humiliating! My life is **OVER**.

Whoa.
You've got three friends now. We've got your back.

And your front.

I bet nobody even noticed. I have more pads in my locker.
Let's get some lunch.

I'll meet you guys at the table... I have something I want to take care of.

Why are the pad dispensers in the bathroom empty?

Excuse me?
My friend just had an emergency, and the machine was empty.

Did you check all the bathrooms?
Um.
No.

BUT STILL! The 30s hall one was empty. I'm guessing they all are. Why? Why aren't they stocked? What if it's an emergency? Where is the nurse?!

RING RING
We don't have a nurse.

Budget cuts all around.

You should get to class, young lady.

Fine.

That night...

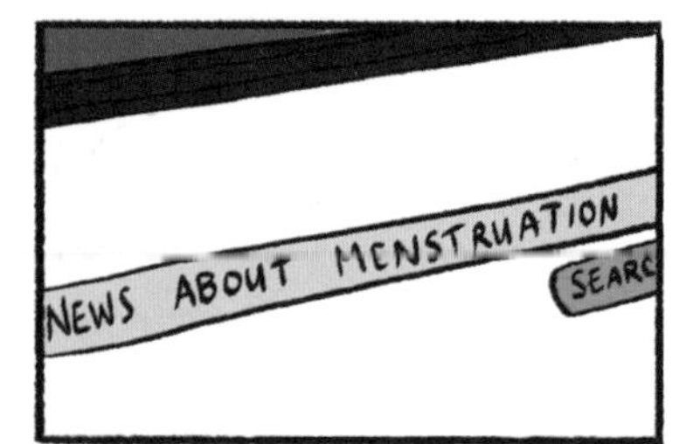
NEWS ABOUT MENSTRUATION

ALL
20,000,0

She couldn't afford tampons, so she used socks. The story of how one woman's plea to a local city council went unheard until now. Next at ten.

BODY AUTONOM
ERIODS AND POLITICS
TAMPON TAX
10 PERIOD HORROR STORIES YOU WON'T WANT TO MISS
FIRST PERIOD STORY
MEN WHO MENSTRUA
WHAT TO KNOW
PELVIC PAI
AND PERIODS
PERIOD TALK IN PUBLIC?
THE FIRST FRONTIER IN FEMINISM: PERIODS
WHAT IS
ADENOMYOSI
DONATE MENSTR
RODUCTS TO SHE
T THE WOMAN WH
NIC TAMPON COMP
SO WHAT'S
MENSTRUAL
TEN PEOPLE
FREE
BLED IN PUBLIC
HOW
PERIOD
OOD OUT OF CLOTHING
MENSTRUATION FACTS
AT WILL MAKE YOU
RSECTION
STRUATI
THIS HOMELESS WOMAN ASKED
STORE FOR A TAMPON AND YOU
WHAT HAPPENE

I'm SO ANGRY!!!
This new girl at school got her period and we were all in the bathroom and the pad machine was empty. She was wearing white pants and it was EVERYWHERE. I felt so bad for her. But then I started thinking, WHY IS THE MACHINE ALWAYS EMPTY?! WHY IS THERE EVEN A MACHINE IF THEY DON'T BOTHER TO FILL IT?! I went to the office but Ms. Carr would barely talk to me about it.
First of all, this is a total injustice!
But second of all...why are people so weird about talking about periods? It's natural. Fifty percent of the population gets a period... but it's like this HUGE secret we can't talk about? That makes no sense!
I've been reading about it since I got home. It seems the same everywhere... Even worse in other countries. Nobody wants to talk about it. I wish there was a way to open the conversation.
I wish periods weren't shameful.

Sasha?

What happened?

Oh,
Uh...

I guess
I, uh...

got my
period.
My friend
gave me a few
extra pads.

Oh.

CLICK

6:30

MAXI

SUPER PLUS!
MAXI
PADS

26
SUPER PLUS

INSERTION INSTRU
ANGLE IT IN
1
2

Sasha! Breakfast!

Christine:
Abby's after school tonight—
homework sesh?
Sasha:
YES! C u there.

MAXI

Christine, did you get an answer for number six?

Not yet.

Hmm, okay. Let me know if you do. I am stuck on the integral.

Yeah, let me know too.

Just kidding. I'm still in Algebra 1...

Brit, do you have a minute to help me with this?
④ 4+√10x=14
√10 x=14-4
10x =10
X=1
⑤ 21-√12x=15

Oh, you forgot to take the square root.

Ohhhhhhhh.

Sasha, you're being really quiet. You okay?

Um, well...
I dunno.

Oh, don't tell us.
It's not like we are your only friends or anything.

CHRISTINE!

Sigh

You guys, this girl from cross-country walked by me today and called me "Bloody Mary" in front of all of her friends. I don't think I can live this one down...

What?
Who??
I bet it was Haven Montez. Or maybe Melly Johnson. They don't know when to quit.

Ugh, just ignore them. I bet no one else even remembers.

I remember...

You'll be yesterday's news soon.

I mean...

At least you didn't *poop* your pants!

Oh my God, Christine.

What?

I'm not wrong.

Hey, guys, speaking of...
Can I...
ask you a kind of awkward question?

Those are my favorite kind.

Shoot.

How the heck are these supposed to work exactly?

I mean...I read the instructions, but seriously? I don't think I can do that.

Oh yeah, tampons are totes weird at first.

They can be lifesavers, though!

Mmm, Life Savers.

SWAT

I remember the first time I tried putting one in.

It just has a big learning curve.

I mean, I don't wear them on my painful cramp days.

But usually you don't even realize it's in there. You just have to remember to change it.
Okay... but...

Have you ever taken out a dry tampon?

You can also just use pads. It's whatever floats your boat.
It's not like anyone would know either way.

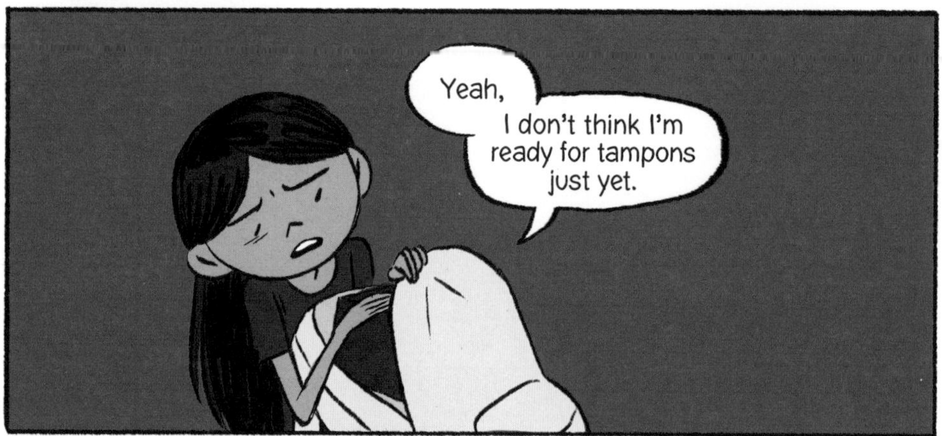
Yeah,
I don't think I'm ready for tampons just yet.

I can tell you what I'm ready for: some of your mom's brownies, Abby!

Think they're out of the oven?

SNIFF
SNIFF

They smell so good!

So, have you guys heard about Toxic Shock Syndrome?

CAM
Alby
Jane Eyre

Some of
you will create a
red solution...

hahaha
and some of
you will create a
yellow solution.
hehehe

I think we know
which one Sasha
will be getting.

ha ha
ha

hahaha

hehe
he
he
ha
haha
haha
ha
HA
HAHA
HAH

That is enough, everyone. Go sit at the lab tables. Pick your partners yourselves.

Roll
Roll

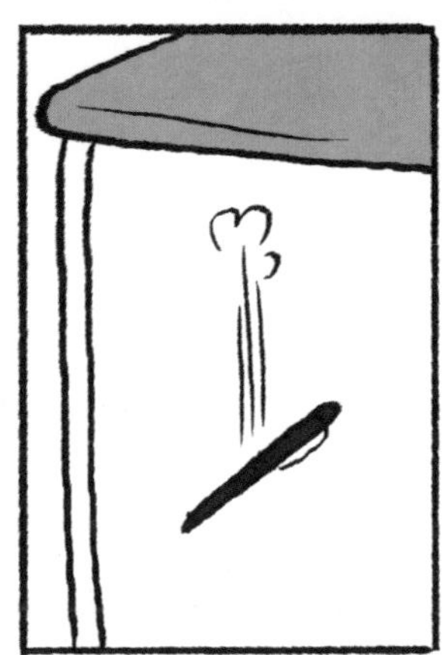

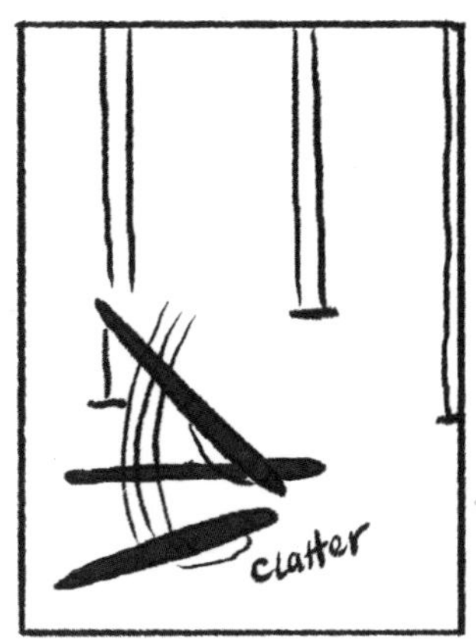
clatter

Um. Excuse me?

I think you dropped this.

Thanks.

So.

Do you have a lab partner yet?

Because I'm new and I don't know anyone and so I was thinking we could, erm, maybe be—

YES!
Please.

I mean...

Okay!
Sure.

October 8
So.

Do you
guys, like...

have
boyfriends?

Ha! I wish!
But you don't see any Darcys around here.

BRIT.

He is fictional...

and ancient.

Darcys?

Brit has an obsession with *Pride and Prejudice*.

Keira Knightley version.
Obvi.

What I mean is there's not really a lot of prospects around this place.

I don't know.

Some guys are kind of cute...

but they seem to be interested in being popular and dating the "cool" girls. Anyone with a different kind of vibe doesn't seem to register.

Maybe it's too much to ask for a fifteen-year-old boy to be interested in anything but sports and hookups.

I dunno. Maybe I'm wrong.

I don't know... Seems like there are an awful lot of guys here. There have got to be some good ones.

Well...there are some really nice ones.
And some smart ones. But honestly, it's hard to find the combo.

What about him?

MATTHEW CARTER?!

HAHAHAHAHAHAHA

He picked his nose through the entire fourth grade. One time he even wiped a booger on my chair.

Okay, maybe not ***him***! But what about him?

Oooh. You can't date him.

?!

He smells like cheese.

And not the good kind.

RING
RING RING

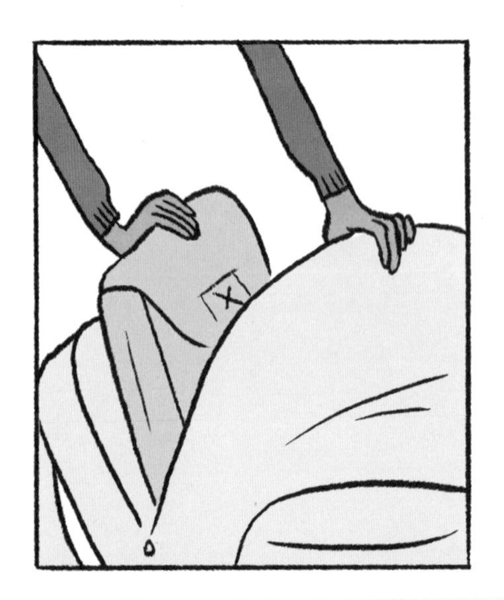

GASP

BLOODY
MARY

BLOODY
MARY

PLUCK

All right, who did this?!
Not cool, people.

So.

Not.

Cool.

MARY

I'm the next Matthew Carter.

HOMECOMING week
FRI - DANCE
MON - QUAD LUNCH
WED - ice cream social
FRI - Rally + game

They're in Brit's room.

Stop squirming.

Howdy.

Hi!

H.H.S.

EMPTY

UNbelievable! Nothing here.

Chill, Abs.

It's a dance. Enjoy yourself for once.

I'm trying.

That's mah girl.

What do you mean, "trying"?

This is the best night of my life!

We look amazing!

The guys of Hazelton don't know what they're in for.

That night...

yawn

Your blog post is live.
CLICK

A blog about menstruation. Period.

Period History

Hi, followers!

I'm back, and I can't stop thinking about periods. So I have been doing some research to see how menstruators have handled it throughout history.

Women!

HISTORICAL PERIOD NONSENSE

+ Back in AD 79, Pliny the Elder of Rome had a whole list of things women could destroy if they came into contact with them while menstruating. He died in the famous Mount Vesuvius explosion (I wouldn't be shocked if he thought a woman caused that...).
+ Women through time and across the world have been isolated during their periods, and some cultures even require women to change their hygiene routines—you know, to cleanse themselves from period evil and all that.

HISTORICAL PERIOD AWESOMENESS

+ In North America, menstruating women were seen as powerful, and many societies were much more equal. How cool is that?! Then the Europeans arrived and things changed…
+ In WWI, the bandages used on soldiers were found to be better at absorbing blood than cotton. Then—BAM! We had disposable pads, which were a game changer for women (who had previously worn rags).
+ In the 1930s, the first patent for the tampon was registered, and by WWII, women in the workforce changed periods forever!

Belts
Pads
Tampons
Cups

Sometimes I wonder how different it would all be if women weren't the ones having periods. Obviously, women aren't the only ones who menstruate—trans men and gender nonconforming people menstruate too, but—it's the fact that women have historically done it that makes it the problem. Overall women have been considered second-class citizens to men. You know, the patriarchy and all that (barf).

As Gloria Steinem said in "If Men Could Menstruate," "Men would brag about how long and how much."

XO,
Abby

+ 6 new followers

Hey, guys!
Oh, wow, 18 is cute! And 25 isn't so bad.
18! I like the tight end with the tight end.
Wink wink.

Sasha! He's a wide receiver.
Isn't the objectification of the male specimens antifeminist?

WOO!
Go 18!

Is it just me or did they get new uniforms?

I overheard that they didn't just get new uniforms...

they got new equipment too.

Hey, my dudes.
Um...

Why did you think consuming that much soda was a good thing, Chris?

Empty. Again.

Hey! Quit fixating!

Hey! Pee faster.

Fifty cents? Who even carries around quarters? Who's going to have that on hand if it's an emergency?

The more I think about it, the more I think this is a real health issue. The school can buy brand-new uniforms for the football team, but they're charging us fifty cents for tampons that they can't even bother restocking?

How are we supposed to focus on school if we're worried about leaking through our pants? Like what if our period just appears and then—***BAM!*** We're caught like Sasha?

No offense, Sasha.
Don't remind me.

You're right, though... Why do the boys get new uniforms again?
We're not asking for a lot here. Just basics.

But how do we get them to pay attention?

Maybe we just have to be louder?

November 6

Abby, the principal will see you now.

Why are we meeting today, Abby?

I am here today...

to discuss the topic of menstruation with you. Specifically, the lack of products stocked at any given time in our bathrooms.

So you are just saying we need to restock the machines?

Well...

not completely. The machines are always empty, but we shouldn't have to pay for them.

How else would we buy the supplies?
It's not like the school has extra money just lying around...

The football team just got new uniforms and equipment.

I asked Coach Mackey and he says they were replaced two years ago!
PRINCIPAL NOTES
① healthcare

Menstruation is a health issue.

And this is an issue that affects over half of our school.

What do you want me to do about it?

We want the machines to be stocked.
PRINCIPAL

And ideally they would be free.

It's not in our budget.

The district has rules on how we spend money.

These products aren't always in the budget for your students either!
Maybe you can petition the district to listen.

I'm sorry, but there is not much I can do for you at this point.
Sir, this is a humanitarian issue. I don't think you are listening to me.

I assure you, I am listening. My hands are tied.

Sir.

This conversation is over. If you really feel passionately about this, you can come to me again next year.

SLAM!

Go get some lunch, dear. The period is almost over.

December 10

I have so much homework and art to do this weekend, I might collapse from exhaustion.

I might collapse on the ice rink.

Blurf.
I have to do homework again with Ted tomorrow.

You sure are spending a lot of time with Ted and his tiny shorts lately.

It's not like...

SO!

I was thinking, we should seriously petition the school.
Just write some letters and send them to the admin.

What do you say?

Um.

That sounds good.

Sweet. I will organize it so it is super easy.
Okay.

Easy.

Hey there, twinkle toes.

Hi.

So.

I heard what Brit said.

You have been hanging out with Ted a bunch lately.

UGHHHHHH

It's so not like that.

It's okay if it is.

But it isn't.

He is just Ted.

And we just have a group project together.

Don't let the romance twins make this into anything it isn't.
Ha ha ha

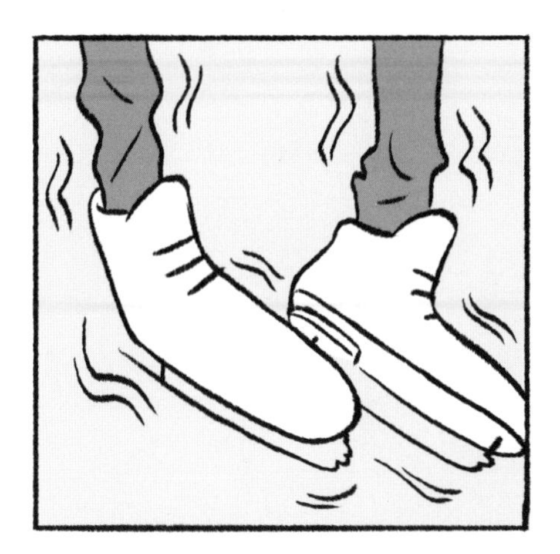

Yay! I'm officially not the worst.

Saturday, December 14
Mom, did you order pot stickers?

They should be under the fortune cookies, Abs.

So how is your piece coming along for the library show?

I dunno.
I think okay?
I can never tell.

How come?

I just feel like...

I want to say a lot, but when I draw it, it is just a drawing and doesn't say a lot.
I know a picture is worth a thousand words and whatever...but I want to actually make change.
This little drawing in the library isn't going to change the way people think about feminism.

Abs, it's Saturday night. Try to relax a little? Think about other things.
But I know your art is going to change the world someday.
You have to say that because you're my mom.

I don't have to say that!

But it's true.

You can doubt yourself all you want, but you have a powerful voice.

You don't know that.
I believe it. You just have to prove it.

That's the problem! I don't know how to prove it!
Abby, you will learn.
Not every issue needs to be solved today.

Is there more soy sauce in the bag?

Okay, we can change the topic...

The next morning...
Here.

What do you think she is going to have us—

YOU GUYS!!!
3

Look what I got!

Look what I did!

What am I looking at here?

Okay. So I thought we would write letters. I got the addresses of every single administrator for the school district.

The school board members, our representatives, cool teachers' home addresses.

AND our senators!

You guys will need some energy.

Hey! Sorry I'm late, the door was open so I—

Wait.
What did I miss?

So...

It seems that we are hand-writing letters? Lots of letters.

About free tampons and pads?

In the public school restrooms?

One question...

You ***have*** heard of e-mail, right?

E-mail would be way too easy for Abby.

When my mom was in college, she used to go to marches and protests and do letter-writing campaigns. She told me about it!

Look, just hear me out.

Anyone can click delete on an e-mail. So we are going old-school! They will have to open these letters and figure out what to do with them!

I think this will really make an impact!

THESE COOKIES ARE GREAT, SHARON!

Sheroes

Tonight I got together with my three friends and we wrote letters to our school board members and the admin of our high school urging them to make pads and tampons available for students in need. When I think about doing things like this, it reminds me of all the women and activists whose shoulders we stand on. That is the coolest thing about fighting for equality: many different voices, socioeconomic backgrounds, races, religions, and more are changing the landscape. Each of those life perspectives adds something unique to the fight.

Here are a few amazing female activists who I look to for strength!

Eleanor Roosevelt—One of the most influential female figures in history and a former First Lady of the United States of America, Eleanor Roosevelt campaigned for human rights on a global scale.

Coretta Scott King—Starting in the '50s, Coretta Scott King was a leader of the civil rights movement and a sought-after speaker (she was the first woman to deliver the Class Day address at Harvard!) who started the Martin Luther King Jr. Center for Nonviolent Social Change and campaigned to make her husband's birthday the national holiday we now recognize as Martin Luther King Jr. Day.

Gloria Steinem—Since the start of her journalism career in the '60s, Gloria Steinem has published a variety of feminist literature from articles to books and even started *Ms.* magazine and the Women's Media Center.

Maya Angelou—The Grammy-winning poet, Pulitzer Prize–nominated writer, accomplished author of thirty-six books, civil rights activist, and Presidential Medal of Freedom winner made such an impact on civil rights by using her art and voice, it is hard not to be inspired by her wisdom!

Malala Yousafzai—Malala has been working to further the rights of girls' education. After surviving an assassination attempt where she was shot in the head, she continues to further children's right to education in the face of danger and was awarded the Nobel Peace Prize at just seventeen years old!!

Signing off for now… I have an art show tomorrow!

XO,
Abby

Comments:

S. Sinclair: I look up to you, my darling daughter! - Mommy

A. Luna: Alexandria Ocasio-Cortez! She is fierce!

ANON: Billie Jean King paved the way for me as a little girl who loved sports.

ANON: You should check out Kiran Gandhi and Nadya Okamoto!

+ 17 new followers

January 3

ABBYSINCLAIR
Whoa!
I knew Abs was good, but this...
This is legit!

Well, I mean, it's still just in a library.

It's still legit.

ABBY SINCLAIR
HONORABLE MENTION

Hi.

You guys, come look at this stuff.

Tuesday,
January 14th

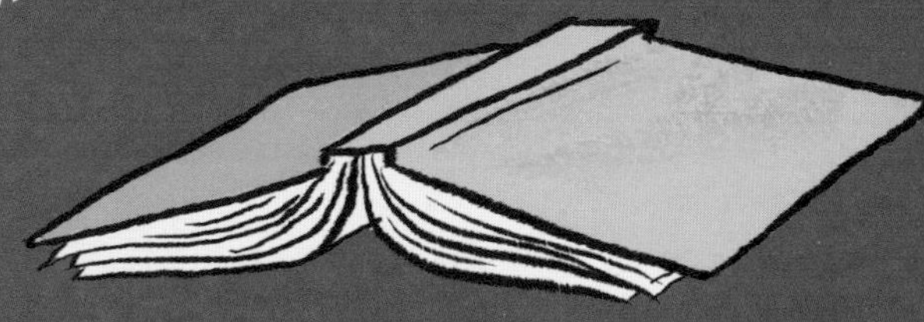

So.

My dad should be here soon.

Righty-oh. I wish my dad picked me up at school.

We could always give you a ride if you want. So you don't have to take the bus.

Oh, I don't want to impose.

Okay, never mind.

Hey, look. There's something I've been wanting to—

Erm. Right.
So I was thinking, since we get on so great in lab...
Maybe we can take our... chemistry...outside the classroom?

Huh?
I'm rubbish at this...

But I was thinking maybe we could go out sometime?
You mean, like...on a date?

Yeah!
Right.
That!

YES!

Brilliant! Well, then...I'll text you?
Sasha!

Okay! Got to go!

Who is that, Sasha?

That's, um...just some boy...
From my class. I think he likes me.

Oh!

Well...um...

Mom doesn't know!
Please don't tell her!

RING
RING
RING

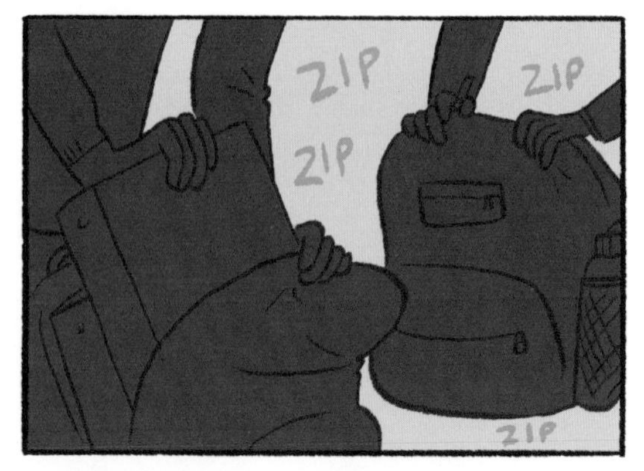
ZIP
ZIP
ZIP
ZIP

Have a great night, and I will see you tomorrow.
Don't forget to grab the homework on the way out!

Hey, Brit,
do you have a minute?

Sure, I'm just writing down the homework.

I wanted to talk to you about all the school you've been missing lately. Are you okay?
Everything okay at home?

Oh yeah. I'm fine.

You are one of the best students. I just want to make sure you aren't falling behind.
Am I falling behind?

No. It's always a concern when students are absent a lot.
Oh.
You know we have counselors if you ever need to talk. My door is always open as well.

Oh...no.
It's not that. It's, um...
I get a lot of headaches.

You should bring a doctor's note in to the office, then.

Okay, I will look into it.

If you get a lot of headaches, have you ever tried pinching your hand right here?

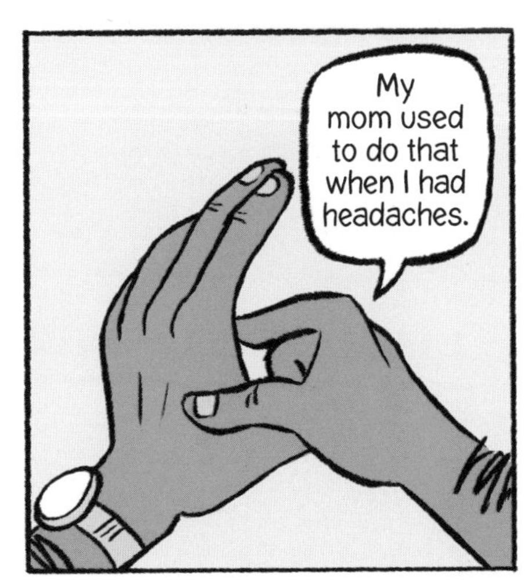
My mom used to do that when I had headaches.

I will definitely try that next time.

Mr. Patel was wondering why I miss class so much. I felt awkward, so I lied and said it was headaches and not cramps...

And...did
it help your
"headaches"?

So much!
My cramps
are gone
now.

Dude, this
could be it. If only
you pinched your hand
every month, then
you'd solve your
problems.

Tell me about it!
Ha ha
ha

Thursday,
February 13th

I feel like we need to be doing more. Like, I talked to the principal, we wrote letters, I had my art show...and yet it's February... and there's been no progress.
Frozen
More?! What more?

I dunno... just more. Change isn't happening!

The ball is in their court, duder.

I'm tired of waiting. We need action.

These things don't move fast, Abby...

I mean, there could be a girl at school we don't even know who needs us to be acting on this faster and more! What if we are letting her down?

You've done everything you can do. Maybe it's time for a little break?

I get it. I know I've been fixating on this. But we're not asking a lot. We are just asking for change in one school. How long could that take?
Change is slow. We're still using an overhead projector in trig, so...

I guess.
I just hate feeling helpless here.

I know you do.

You ever notice how chocolate fro-yo looks identical to the poop emoji?

God, you're embarassing sometimes!

Abs, answer the question!

Oh my Gawwwd, Christine!
Don't look now, but Haven and Ted and their little posse are approaching.

Hey, dude!

OGURT
Sup?
Fro-yo.

Noice.

Word.

Let's go, Ted.

Later.

What?

Hey, are you guys ready to go?

Sure, let's get out of here!

SHOTGUN!

No fair! You got it last time!

Christine, you are so sticky right now.

I don't want your hands on the radio.

Come on, Brit! I called it. That's a serious injustice.
Doesn't your mom get to decide anyway? She's the one driving!

Abby gets shotgun.

Wednesday, February 19
GO!

GO!
FASTER!
GO!
GO!
GO!
STROKE!
GO!

GO! GO GO!
GO! GO!
GO!

GOOOO!

GO! GO!

ALMOST THERE!

And that is Schmidt at the wall first for Hazelton High!

YES!
AHHH!

High fi—

We have that test Monday...

can I help you study?

Uh... In trig?

For sure. I'll text you!

Dude! Let's go!

But...I have a 104 percent in trig...

Saturday,
February 22nd

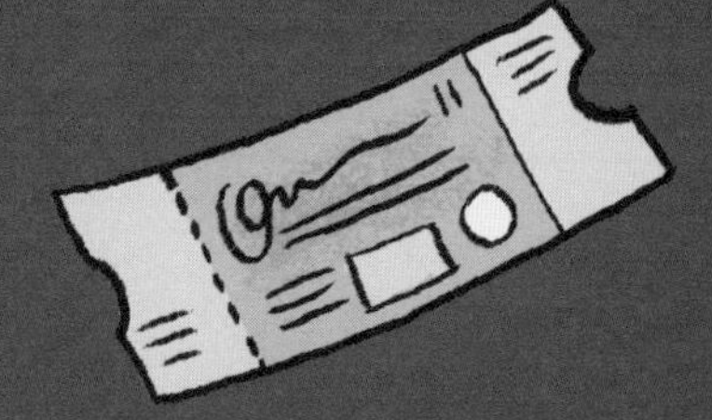

and he was like Ooooh Oh That's what I wanna dooo

DING DING
3:00
TOM

Thomas: Hey what's up?

Sasha: Nothing much. Just homework! How r u?!
Thomas: I was thinking if you're not busy, maybe we could catch a movie tonight. 8:00, I'll pick you up?

New
5:00
8:00
9:00

You're from England, right?

Yup! Merry olde.

Huh?

What's England like?

It seems so posh and dignified and...and... I mean, Harry Potter is, like, my favorite, ever! Did you go to boarding school and, like, wear uniforms?

Ha ha, nope. Just regular secondary school with uniforms.
Secondary?

That's what we call high school in England. You said this is your first year at Hazelton too, yeah?
Yeah, my mom got a new job, so the whole family moved from Sacramento.

Do you miss your old school? And friends?

Mostly my friends. Everything's so different here...but it's also kind of exciting? I mean, I think I'm getting the hang of this place...
What about you? Do you miss Sacramento?
Yeah. I really like some of the people I've met, but I guess I really miss...just, like, feeling like I belong, you know?
I miss feeling comfortable.

I know the feeling... well.
Maybe we can figure out this Hazelton High thing together?

What do you think?

Sounds like a plan.

this SUMMER

Monday,
March 2nd

WRITE
explore!

DAVIS
live APRIL 14 1963

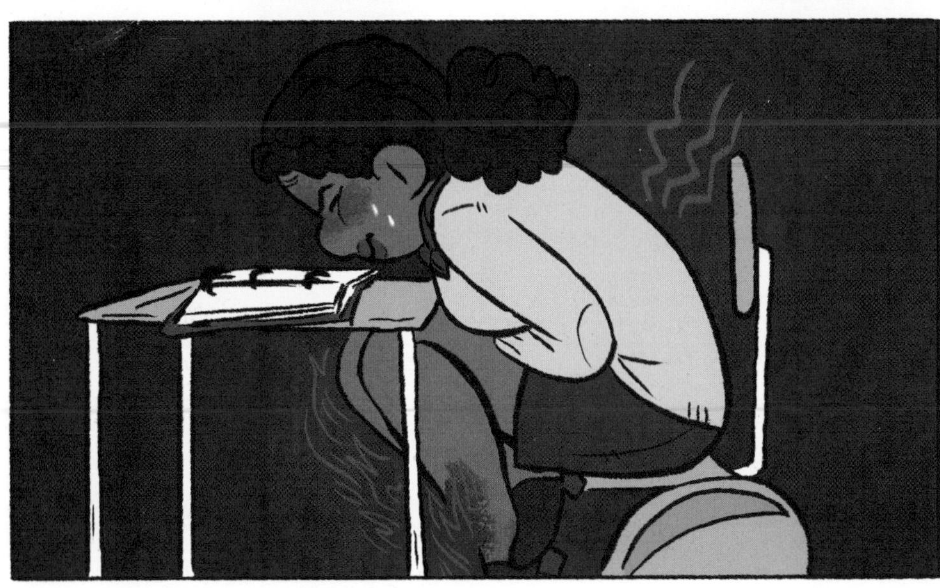

May I go to the restroom?
Yes, Brit.

Why is she leaving with her whole backpack?

CLICK

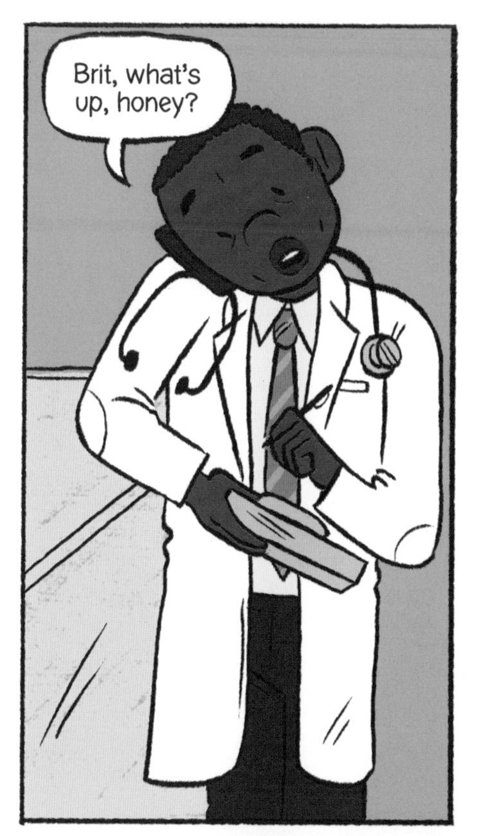
Brit, what's up, honey?

Dad, I need to come home.

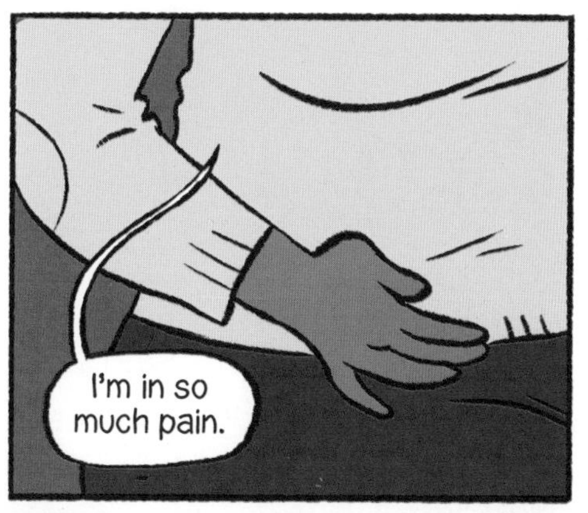
I'm in so much pain.

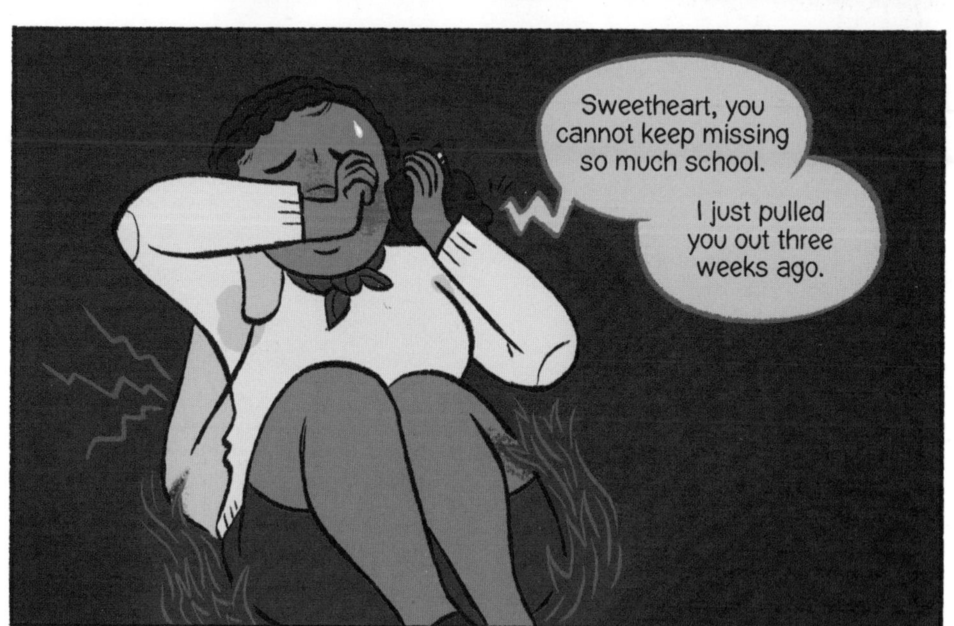
Sweetheart, you cannot keep missing so much school.
I just pulled you out three weeks ago.

I know, Dad, but it hurts **SO** much.
I feel like I could be sick at any moment.

What did Dr. Maganti say to you again?
There's nothing to do. I took my painkillers like she said to.

I just want to lie down.

Okay, honey. I will be there in fifteen minutes.

Tuesday,
March 3rd

DING
DONG

Christine, honey, I let Ted in.
Thanks, Gram.
Hey, Ted.

Gram, we're going to study in the living room.

Ted, are you staying for dinner? I was going to reheat some stroganoff.

Oh, no, thank you, ma'am. My mom told me I had to be home for dinner.

Suit yourself, dear.

Where are your books, dudenoffski?

Why don't we go get ice cream?

What?
We're both eating dinner later...

I thought you wanted to study.

I mean, we could...

or we could do something else...

I don't think that...

It's just that...

I'm not really interested in...

Oh, this is awkward.
You thought I was asking you out?

I couldn't ever like someone like...you.

But you were the one—

Bye, Gram. I actually have to take off.

Ted! What the...

Honey, what was that?
DOOR SLAM

It's nothing.
I don't...

Christine.

The women in this family march to the beat of their own drum.

Yeah.

Wednesday,
March 4th

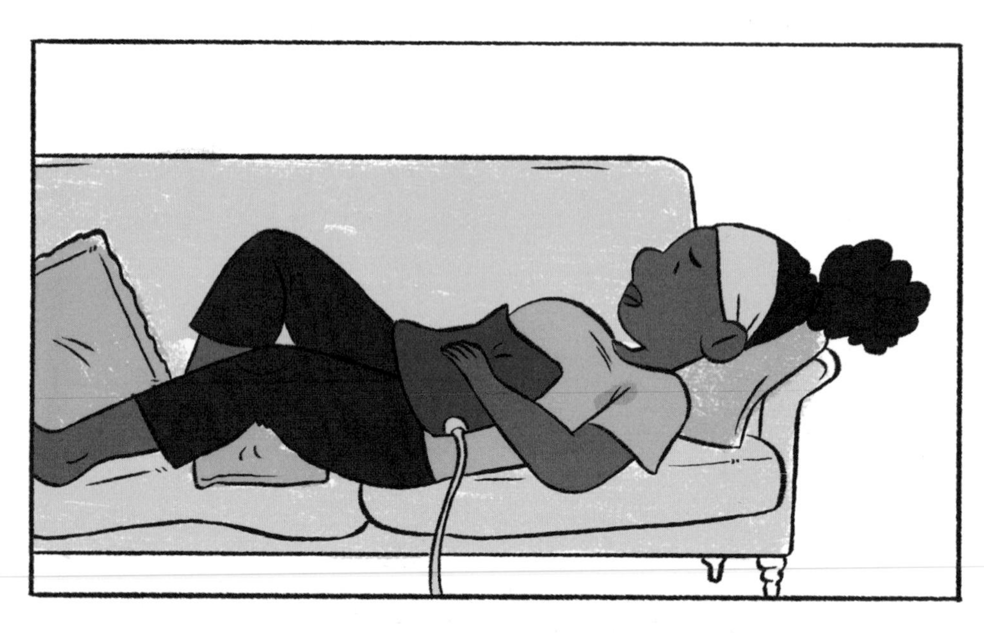

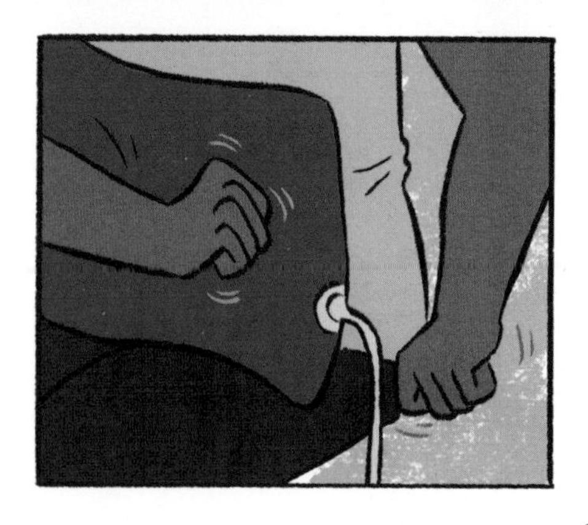

Hey, honey.

I brought you some chocolate.

My doctor said I shouldn't eat much sugar when I'm on my period.

Well...your mom says you need a little.

I love you.

I know.

Why is this happening to me?

Why am I always in so much pain?

You are just one of those people, my girl.
I don't want to be one of those people.

I know, honey.
But Dad is looking into finding you an endometriosis specialist, someone who can do a proper exam and who specializes in excision.

Yeah, I know.

Mom, did I, like...do something bad in a former life?
Honey, I don't think you should think like that.

It doesn't seem fair.

It's *not* fair.
Maybe this is the burden you bear for being so smart?

Mooooom!

I'm kidding.

I *am* smart, though.

You are very smart.

And kind.
And strong.

What if...

Never mind.

What?

What if...

What if there's actually something wrong with me?

Honey girl, we will figure this out.
Together.

But what if we don't?

We will.
Let's start with this specialist Dad is finding you and go from there.

Okay.

I know we will get to the bottom of this.

Spaghetti for dinner?

Sounds good.

Hiiiiiii!

Hey.

Are you feeling any better?! You haven't been at school.

Ugh. Not really. I'm just so sick of my periods.
I'm sorry, Brit. It just isn't fair that you have such crappy periods.

It just sucks. Hard.
Yeah... I bet.

Sasha? What if there's something really wrong with me?

I'm sure if there is, they'll find it.

I'm just really scared.
But you can't be the only person going through this, right? I mean, you're not, like, a medical anomaly or something!

I think it's probably just, like, really hard to not be scared when you feel like you're always in pain.

Yeah, it is.

Your periods make mine look like I don't even have a period!
Ha ha, totally!

I don't know if I could, like, even handle that. You—

Hey, Sasha?

Yeah?

What if...

I can't have kids?

OMG!

Well, I would have them for you.

Sasha!
For reals.

What are friends for if you can't use them for surrogacy?

ha ha ha ha
ha ha
A lot of other things!

I really would have kids for you, Brit.

I'm so glad you got your period that day and we found you.

You have no idea how glad I am.

Ha ha ha
I'm pretty sure I am way happier about that whole situation.

Well, now you're having my kids, sooo...

True.

I guess we're even!

So then Ted runs out of the room! Just like that.

Odd.

Are you even listening to me?

I'm kind of worried Ted and I aren't friends anymore.

Earth to Abs!

I'm listening.

It's not like you're best friends. I'm sure he's got other prospects. I mean, he can't be that crushed, right?
Gee. Thanks.

You know what I mean. Maybe it's not that big of a deal.
I mean, you didn't like him, right? At least not in that way.

Definitely not.

See? I'd be more worried if you liked him like that and then he ran away.

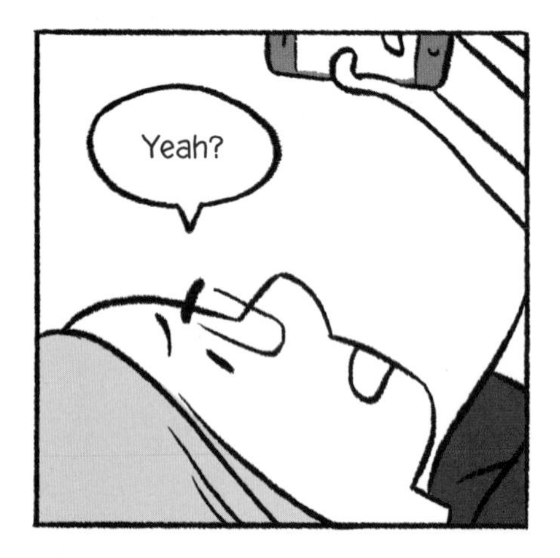
Yeah?

I'm not sure I feel that way for any guy.

Not the way I feel about you.

Huh?

I mean you guys—you, Brit, and Sasha.

Well, yeah, we are all really close.
Mm-hmm.

Anyway, he is such a bro. He won't be hung up for long.

It's just that he was acting so weird.

I guess you're right, though.
Maybe it will just blow over and things will go back to normal.

Yup. Good old status quo.

Yeah, status quo.

Is there anyone you think is...

cute?

I have other stuff on my mind right now.

Yeah? What's up with you lately, anyway? You're so angry.

Oh!
Sasha and Brit just came on!

What's up, compadres?

Did you hear about how Layke asked MacKayla to prom?

Was that the one where he rented a goat and was like, "Will you *goat* to prom with me?"

Oh my God, how embarassing.

No, Layke asked MacKayla by mowing "PROM?" into her parents' lawn.

If Tom did that in front of my mom, I'd die!

If your prom-posal is that big...what do you do when you want to get engaged?
Good point.
I just want something really romantic.

But super personal. Just cute and silly and only between us.

Right? Same.

I dunno, seems kinda cool to go all out.

Out of all of us, I would never expect that from you.

Well, like...

Isn't it better to make an impact than to be forgettable?

Really?

Go big or goat home.

Right?

Go big or go home...
You know...

I think I have to go.
Bye, guys.

Go big
or go
home.
Go big or go home.

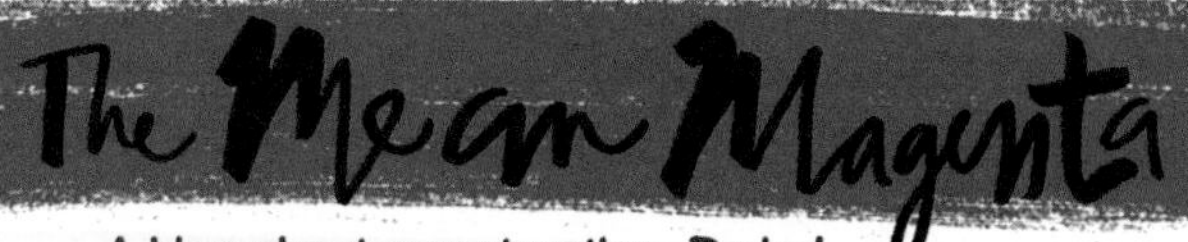

A blog about menstruation. Period.

Go BIG or Go Home

You have to go big to make an impact.

And I want to make an impact.

XO,
Abby

The next day...

...and then I was like... "Wait, what do you think biscuits are?"

Oh no...

So then Thomas goes, "In England, 'biscuits' means 'cookies.'"

hahaha
ha haha

PORT
our
EDERS

So I had brought those peel-and-puff biscuits!

That is too good!

gasp

Oh no.

TELL US ABOUT
YOUR PERIOD
just happened!
I ♥ TAMPONS!
short!
long &
heavy

PERIODS are N
period stigma hurts us ALL!
PMS is REAL!
DID YOU KNOW?
Period BLOOD USED TO BE USED AS MEDICINE!
PERIODS
ARE BLO
AWE

BLEEDING
IS
NORMAL

RIOD
WER!

Oh no.
Oh no.
Oh no.

Huh.

Hi!

Abby.
This...

What the *FUDGE* is this?!

What?!

Why didn't you talk to us about this before, Abby?

UPPORT
EEDERS
all
I thought you guys would like this.
I went rogue. I'm making them notice, right?

Too rogue. Way too rogue.
You didn't consult us.
Yeah! What the heck! This is too aggro, Abs.

We have to make them listen!
They aren't listening.

We go to public school! Did you know there are kids here who can't even afford lunch? How can they afford proper sanitary items for their periods if they cannot afford lunch?! I want to help them. We *need* to help them!
Why does no one care like I care?!

Listen, we care.

But we didn't want to be...

How *could* you?!

I didn't mean to...

SOB

I am going to go...

Look. Your heart is in the right place. I can feel that it is.

This just isn't how to convince people to make change, Abs. This makes people mad at you. We didn't want anyone to be mad at us. We just wanted to survive Hazelton.

Girls.

Wait here.

PRINCIPAL

This is completely inappropriate.

It was me.

Completely me.

Listen, girls. I know you are trying to make a difference and solve your little problem... but you can't fix everything. Especially if you cause property destruction.
It's not like the boys get free jock itch cream.

That's not even the same—
So. What are we going to do?
This certainly isn't acceptable at all. It sends a message. Two days suspension for you, Abby, and a warning to your friends. I don't want to see anything like this happening again. Keep your art projects in the classroom.

Okay?

Okay.

You know I am new here.

You rescued me when I got my period in front of everyone and was mortified.

People already know me as the period girl and the new girl. I don't want any of this.

You really hurt and embarrassed me, Abby.

I just need some time to think about this.

Abby, we know you wanted to help, and we wanted to make a difference with you.

Dude, we are always here for you with that.

We are also just trying to survive high school...and I can't get into trouble like this.

My gram will kill me.

I know your heart was in the right place, Abby.

It's just, like...
SQUEEZE

Do you remember when we were kids and Christine and I wanted to play foursquare at recess every day, but all you wanted to do was sit and draw? You made us draw at recess! We hated it so much, and we got up and left you, just so we could play.

You were so upset you had been ditched, but we just didn't want to draw. You thought we would all be having fun, but really it was just fun for you...
This is... kinda like that.

Yeah...

I'm really sorry.

It's okay. We love you. We're used to your antics.

Do you think Sasha will ever talk to me again?

Probably. Just give her a bit of space. This forced her to relive her most embarrassing day.

You really did go big, didn't you? It's oddly impressive.

Okay, we gotta get to class.

Text us later. Hope your mom doesn't freak out too much.

That Night

TITLE:
BODY:

BODY:

I have three best friends who mean the world to me.

With them at my side, I've spent the entire school year focusing on making a difference and changing people's minds about periods. But today I went too far and I upset my best friends. They have every reason to be mad at me, because I got us all in big stinking trouble.

It's kinda cool how we all have such different periods! My periods are pretty regular. I have some cramps, but nothing too painful, and I bleed for about four days. I consider myself lucky.

When I stumbled into this world of feminism and menstrual equity, I was shocked to learn about period poverty and just how different periods are. I wanted to make a difference for menstrual equity in some way, so I focused on my school...which doesn't stock the sanitary item dispensers in the bathrooms (I know, right?)!

If we aren't even providing resources for girls like me with easy periods, what are we doing for girls whose periods are long, heavy, and painful? Girls with endometriosis, adenomyosis, PCOS, fibroids? What are we doing for our fellow bleeders in poverty?

All of those questions have a simple answer: none of these issues are being addressed because people still think periods are gross. So, I took matters into my own hands. I completely took over the school with period imagery. Think: Period posters, streamers, toilet paper, walls of questionnaires...the whole nine yards.

And I was suspended because of it. I know vandalism is wrong, but everything I did washes away or can be peeled off. I just wanted to talk about periods.

Talking about periods is the first step to taking that period power back.

But I have overstepped and hurt some of my favorite people...and I have talked too much...so right now I'm done talking. I am ready to listen.

I want to hear from you, if you're still out there...

- Abby

TITLE:
BODY:
I have three best friends who mean the world to me.
With them at my side, I've spent the entire school year focusing on making a difference and changing

POST

click
POST

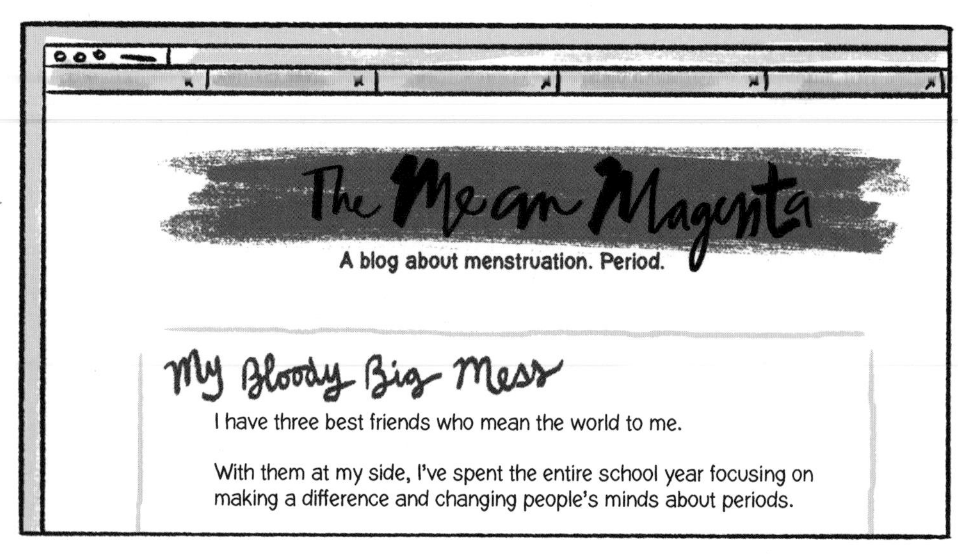
The Mean Magenta
A blog about menstruation. Period.
My Bloody Big Mess
I have three best friends who mean the world to me.
With them at my side, I've spent the entire school year focusing on making a difference and changing people's minds about periods.

Abby, if you are done with your homework, please come here.

Yeah? Coming.

I want you to resolve this with Sasha. You can have your computer, but the minute you are done with this, I am keeping your phone overnight.

Fine.

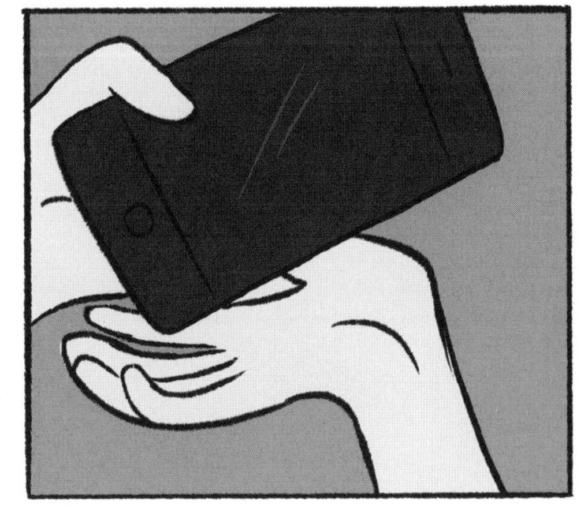

Type Type
Type

Sasha, I wanted to
delete

Hey, Sasha! I thought
* delete, delete *

So I know I majorly messed
delete

gasp

SEND

Beep Beep

Abby: I am really sorry.

Read

I am really sorry.
Read

Read

Sasha: Why?

Abby: I am sorry bcuz I was being selfish. I was so interested in changing the world that i forgot to see how it would affect my closest friends. I didnt even think that this would be sensitive for you and that wasnt ok to overlook. I know i have made things harder for you... I didnt mean to. I feel terrible.
Abby: Sorry for being such a 💩 friend.

Sasha: You were kinda a 💩 friend.
Abby: I totally was.
Sasha: Thanks for saying

Abby: Flow-sure. I feel like a big pile of 💩.

Sasha: I think it's cool what you were trying to do. I just wished you'd warned me or like...
Sasha: let me be part of it in some way.
Sasha: now period stuff just keeps happening to me.
Sasha: That feels so lame.

Sasha: I don't want to be Bloody Mary forever.

Abby: I'm sorry I made it worse. im going to make it up to you.
Sasha: Deal.

Abby:
Sasha:

How did it go?
Good.

10:20

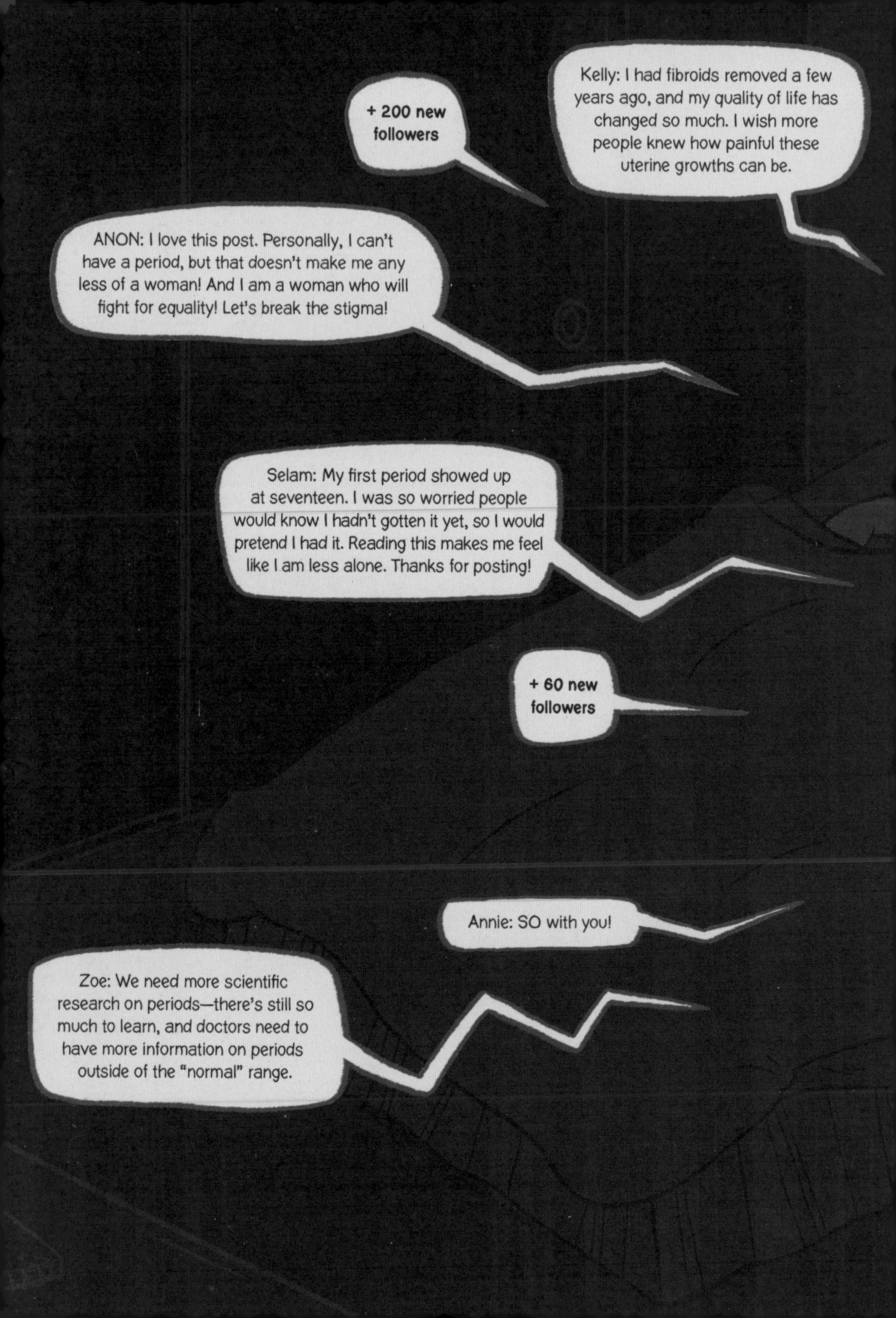

+ 200 new followers

Kelly: I had fibroids removed a few years ago, and my quality of life has changed so much. I wish more people knew how painful these uterine growths can be.

ANON: I love this post. Personally, I can't have a period, but that doesn't make me any less of a woman! And I am a woman who will fight for equality! Let's break the stigma!

Selam: My first period showed up at seventeen. I was so worried people would know I hadn't gotten it yet, so I would pretend I had it. Reading this makes me feel like I am less alone. Thanks for posting!

+ 60 new followers

Annie: SO with you!

Zoe: We need more scientific research on periods—there's still so much to learn, and doctors need to have more information on periods outside of the "normal" range.

Shared 2,000 times

300 likes

Leilani: I have easy periods and they sometimes skip months, but my best friend has really heavy periods.

ANON: I got my first period at nine. It always surprises people, because we think that's too young. But it happens!

Maria: I put tampons in the bathroom at my work sometimes because everyone should be able to bleed without shame.

Mom... Can I have my phone?

It was buzzing like crazy this morning. I don't know how you didn't hear it.

So can I have it?
You were suspended, and now your phone is buzzing up a storm.
No.

You can have it when you are done with your breakfast.

Okay. Done.

THE MEAN MAGENTA
Abby omg check your blog asap
BRIT
omg.
FRONT PAGE OF TRENDFEED!!!!! Now!
SASHA

Christine: I cannot beliebbb you are front page news kid.
btw just walked into a wall while texting that.

RING RING

Hi, Abby! This is Fran from the school newspaper. We want to get a quote from you about your images going viral.

Uh... I'm going to have to call you back.

RING RING

INCOMING
BRIT
CELL

ABBY!!!

We're between classes, but we had to call! **WHAT THE HECK IS GOING ON?!**

Shhh!

FLUSH

Where are you guys?

The crapper.
Now tell us what's up.

I don't really kn—
OH MY GOSH!!! YOU ARE FAMOUS, ABBY! You are ***GLOBAL!!***

Oh my gosh, Sasha! Shhh!
Sorry, sorry, sorry!

What am I going to do now? I haven't even seen this. I haven't opened my computer. I don't know what I am doing.
What if it's bad?
I am really worried this is bad.

What?

The trolls! The trolls will come for me! I'm not ready for the trolls.

I didn't ask for trolls!

hahaha

Whoa okay. Calm down. We're going to help you figure this out, okay? Here's what's going to happen...

Abs, what is going on?
I'm not sure! I think I went viral.

ding!
ding!
ding!
ding!
ding!
ding!
ding!
ding!
ding!
ding!

50 unread e-mails
206,000 shares
33,000 retweets
579,000 likes

Boom Boom Boom Boom

PROTESTING FOR PERIODS? THIS TEEN HAS YOU SPOTTED.
CHANGING THE FLOW: GIRL TRASHES HIGH SCHOOL OVER PERIODS
TEEN TRASHES SCHOOL FOR ACCESS TO PERIOD PRODUCTS
WHAT IS PERIOD POVERTY? THIS GIRL TAKES ON HER SCHOOL TO EXPLAIN
AREA TEEN UPSET OVER HAZELTON HIGH'S ACCESS TO MENSTRUAL HYGIENE
PERIODS ARE TAKING OVER THIS HIGH SCHOOL... LITERALLY!
THIS TEEN WANTS TO END PERIOD POVERTY IN HER HIGH SCHOOL
TEEN SAYS "PERIODS ARE NORMAL!"

Anna: Kids are our future! And the future is here!
Vicky: Abby, if you are reading this: I've loved your art for a long time, but this is so badass!
Paige: ZOMG!
Emily: You are all kinds of crazy! I love it!
Karen: Those teachers have no choice but to listen to her now!
ANON: I love that part where she says her mom's protest stories inspired her lol
Minju: I bet this inspires others!
ANON: I made 5000$ a day working from home! Find out how you can 2...
Kaley: I feel like I want to start talking about my period now too.
Brandt: Uh, this rocks!
ANON: She goes to my school!
Amy: Love!
Jeanne: Oh no! I hope you don't get in trouble. Oh, wait, I just read... You got in trouble.
Ryan: Menstruation is normal! No more shame!

After School

Say: "Tampons should be free and accessible for all!"

Let's start responding to your one million new e-mails!

Help me. I'm so nervous.

I can type if you want!

I think you should say, "I believe that menstruation shouldn't be taboo" not "I want."

Make sure that you include we all did this together. This was our vision.

But you took the fall.

Yeah, but it was our vision. We all get credit for challenging the system.

Why don't we set up a fund-raiser on one of those giving sites?

Like donations?

Oooh! Let's do it! All donations will go toward pads and tampons that we will donate to our school!

District. We need them, but others need them more. Go big, right?

Abby! You know that organic, natural, chemical-free tampon company you love?
Yup.

They read the article about you in TEENnews and want to donate a year's worth of pads and tampons to our school!

You're really doing it, kid!

I'm so proud of you.

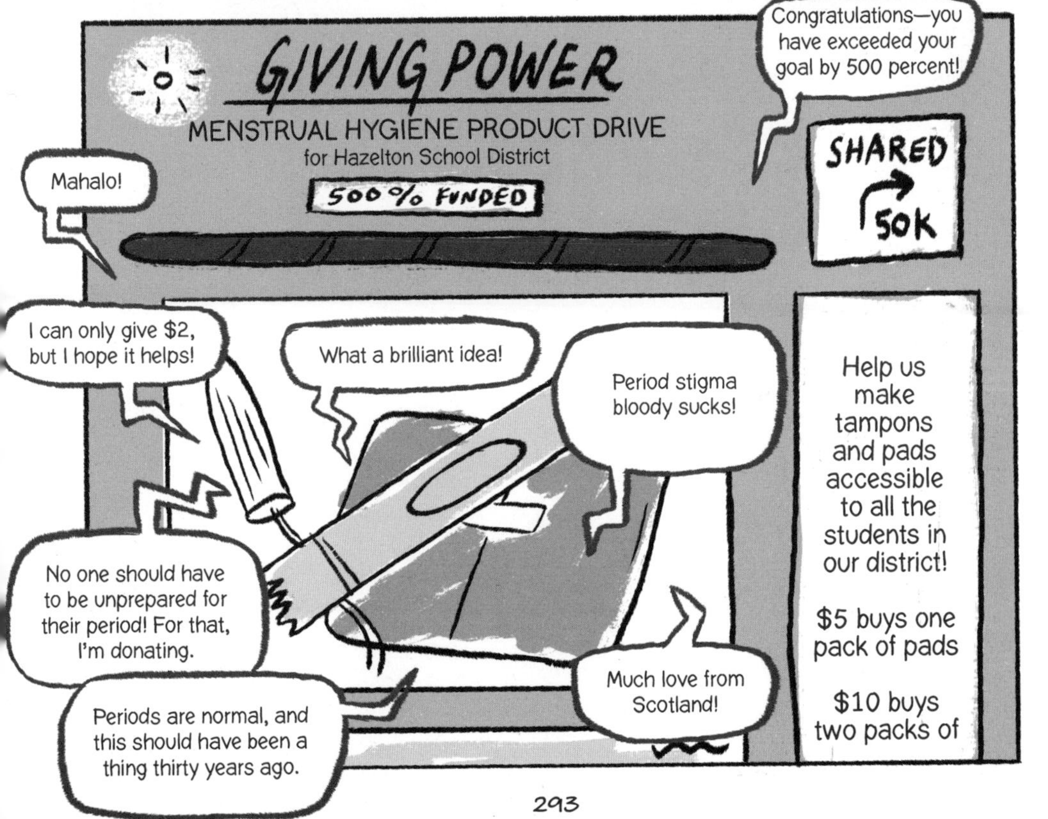
GIVING POWER
MENSTRUAL HYGIENE PRODUCT DRIVE
for Hazelton School District
500% FUNDED
Congratulations—you have exceeded your goal by 500 percent!
SHARED 50K
Mahalo!
Help us make tampons and pads accessible to all the students in our district!
$5 buys one pack of pads
$10 buys two packs of
I can only give $2, but I hope it helps!
What a brilliant idea!
Period stigma bloody sucks!
No one should have to be unprepared for their period! For that, I'm donating.
Much love from Scotland!
Periods are normal, and this should have been a thing thirty years ago.

Monday,
March 9th

You did a really cool thing.
Thank you.

Thanks, Abby. I sent your blog link to my cousin.

You're welcome!

You guys are so gross.

Hey, you guys!

Hello to you. Welcome ba—
WHAT IS THAT?

What's that smell?

It kinda smells like...
BLOOD.

Shut up, Ted.

Sorry about him.

Whatever. It still stinks.

You know what really stinks, Ted?

When someone you think is your friend turns out to be a real bag of farts.

That's you, Ted! You're a giant bag of farts!

WALK AWAY!
Ya big ol' fart bag!

Omg.

Tuesday,
March 17th

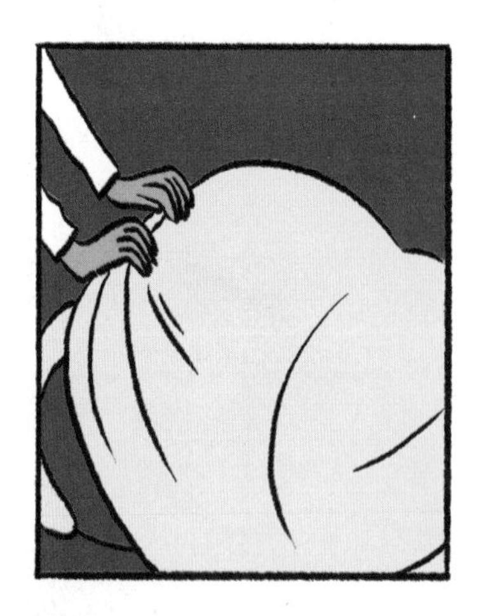

You guyyyyss!

I just had to stay a little late in history, and Mrs. Simmons came in to talk to Mr. Davis and she said that apparently over in the city, the students are getting restless.
They read about what we did here, and some girls just held a walkout for the pads and tampons in the school bathrooms. Mrs. Simmons heard about it from her friend who teaches there!

Whoa! And they said that with you in the room?

Well, I acted all quiet, and then they noticed I was there and asked me to hurry along.

You snoop!

This is wicked cool!
Wow.
Look what we started, Abby!

I mean, technically you started it... We just know how to go with the flow.

Get it? Go. With. The. Flow.
No. We get it.

That is cool, Sasha.
I thought so.

Abs, can I have your cookies?
Sure.

So what's next?
What do you mean?
I mean, we can change lives. That's what we do now, right?

So what's the next thing?

Can we solve the mystery of why I have such bad cramps?
At this point it seems more likely you'll meet Mr. Darcy.

OUUUCH!!

You deserved that.

Whatever.

I want to solve that one too.

Yeah.

It's okay, though. I'm still going to have your kids if you can't have them.
Wait.

Is there something we need to know?
Sasha volunteered to have my children.

Totally normal high school thoughts.

No matter what happens, we'll be there for you, Brit.

I love you guys.

We love you too, woman!

So... what's the next thing?

Well... I do have a couple of thoughts...

Saturday,
March 28th

Come on, it's prom! Just a little mascara.

I don't care if it's your wedding. No mascara.

You are lucky I agreed to come at all.

I want you to look your best!

I always look my best. Besides. I'm wearing ChapStick.

And it's tinted.

But you're my friend date.

Yeah...

BRIT! This dress is a mess! Help!

Where did your mom even find it?

What you need is a belt... Abby, do you have a ribbon?

Of course!

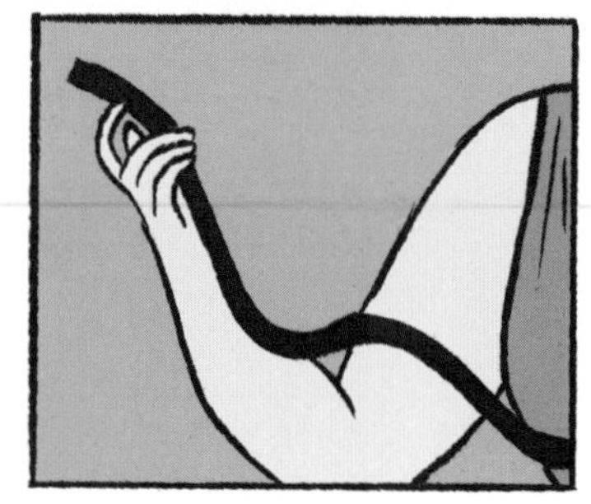

What are you? Mary Poppins? Why do you have a ribbon in your purse?
Emergencies!

I look so pretty!

Yeah, but not as good as me!

I am wearing ChapStick.

We are going to be slowing it down now...
written

night stars you'll be with me forever and eve

STEP

written in the Starsss

ONE TWO THREE FOUR!

SQUEEZE

SLAM

Oh no! Shoot!
Ughhh!

Umm... Does anyone have a tampon?

Thank you.
You're welcome.

Authors' Note

For those of us who have periods, there is a point in every friendship where you start discussing your periods together. Maybe you have experienced that, or maybe you have yet to experience it, but it is definitely a thing. This discussion has allowed those who bleed to create a safe space without judgment to discuss their health. This space has been a saving grace through time, because the majority of people who have their periods are girls and women. Transgender men and gender nonconforming people also have their periods, and this is something important to note, because menstrual health is an issue that affects more than just girls and women. However, because primarily women bleed, periods have historically been a taboo (and even untouchable) topic. Due to sexism that dates back to the dawn of time, periods have typically been seen as something to fear because they are associated with women. It is this stigma around menstruation that makes those of us who have periods discuss it in private, only with each other, and only once we have established that friendship is safe.

This discussion of periods in private has been crucial for protecting women and all who menstruate. It is because of this hushed conversation that we know if our periods aren't "normal" or we know if we are bleeding "too much" or "too little" or maybe, like Brit, our periods seem significantly more painful than our friends'. We are only now starting to discuss periods openly. We chose to start an online comic series called The Mean Magenta based off the idea that women talk about their periods frequently in private. After much brainstorming, we met our girls: Brit, Sasha, Christine, and Abby. We made comics about the things we wished we had known growing up so that the conversation would be approachable. We wanted conversations about periods to be funny, friendly, sometimes embarrassing, and a little annoying. When Macmillan asked us to write a graphic novel about our girls, we could not have been more excited! A fictional book about friendship, centered on periods! What could be better? What could be more needed?

Go With the Flow was born out of our desire to make the book we wished we had had growing up. We wished we had felt more comfortable in our changing bodies at ten, twelve, thirteen, sixteen, and now. We hope that you, dear reader, are able to read about Brit, Sasha, Christine, and Abby figuring out their bodies, their voices, and their periods and know that even through the pain and embarrassment, they are not ashamed.

Periods are funny. Periods are a bit annoying. But mostly...periods are normal.

The more we talk about periods outwardly, the more the stigma around periods shatters. When the stigma is dismantled, we can address more issues with periods and how to achieve period equity around the world. But it starts at home. Bit by bit, we can dismantle the stigma together by talking... and reading. Thank you for picking up this book and reading it—you are helping everyone who has a period just by reading this book.

Flowever yours,
Lily and Karen

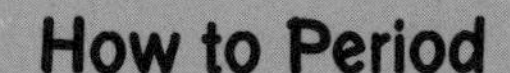

How to Period

There are so many ways to have your period. There is no one correct way! That is the cool thing about having a period. You could get it at age ten or seventeen. You could bleed a lot each month or bleed a little. Or maybe you love tampons, but your friend swears by pads. Or maybe you prefer neither and love your menstrual cup.

However your period goes, go with the flow of it.

What Is Normal?

A good question. And not an easy one to tackle! Hey, Karen here. Growing up, I had very unpredictable periods. I had a science teacher in high school who said that periods follow the moon in perfect twenty-eight-day cycles. This may be true for some people, but could not be any more untrue for me. I could never predict when they'd show up or how long they'd last, so I started wearing liners every day once I'd gone two weeks since my previous period. It was sometimes nerve-wracking and very hard to plan around, but it turns out, that was my normal. I have a few friends with the same type of cycle. Other friends have ovaries that are like clockwork.

Now (after two babies!) my cycle is completely different. Hormonal changes throughout your life will affect your period in a lot of different ways: its duration, timing, even how painful the cramping can be. What's most important to know is what's normal for you. Tracking my period helped me really know what was going on with my body, so I highly recommend getting to know your own personal "normal." There are a lot of free apps you can download to help track the duration, frequency, and any symptoms you experience that may be related to your period. Or just use a regular old journal or calendar. This has been the best way for me to know what is normal and to help me realize when something seems a little off and it may be time to check with a doctor.

Period Pain

Hi! It's Lily here. I am writing to you personally about period pain as someone who has had period pain since my first period at age twelve. For a long time, I thought my pain was maybe just a little more extreme than my friends' pain. But, after talking about it with my peers more and more…I realized, like Brit, that maybe it wasn't as normal as I had thought. In a lot of ways, Brit's period pain story is my story. That is the reason that you don't see her get a diagnosis at the end of the book, because it rarely works out like that. One in ten women has endometriosis, and it takes on average eight to twelve years to get a diagnosis. For me, it took fourteen years. I wasn't actually diagnosed with endometriosis until this book was most of the way finished! While working on *Go With the Flow*, I went to the emergency room for pain related to my uterus and even had endometriosis excision surgery with an endometriosis specialist.

Endometriosis can present in a lot of different ways, including but not limited to extremely bad cramps, backaches, painful bowel movements, fatigue, bloating, constipation, menstrual diarrhea, nausea, pain with exercise, painful urination, sciatic pain, and pelvic pain separately from menstruation. Sometimes people have bad cramps and they go away after their periods, which is often called "dysmenorrhea." What separates dysmenorrhea from endometriosis is that endometriosis is caused by endometrium-like tissue (the stuff that lines your uterus) growing in other parts of the body. It is unclear why and how this happens, but it can present in period havers as early as their first period.

This is why it is important to talk to your friends about your periods. If you are having a period experience that seems too far outside of what your friends are experiencing, see a doctor. If that doctor doesn't take you or your pain seriously, see a different doctor. There can be complications like (but not limited to) polycystic ovaries, endometriosis, adenomyosis, dysmenorrhea, fibroids, and more that need to be addressed by a proper physician (often a specialist). If you or someone you know has painful periods, point them toward Nancy's Nook Endometriosis Education Facebook group, or the Center for Endometriosis Care Website.

The more information that is out there on topics like this, the more those who need it can help themselves. Information is power, and I hope that this information will help someone out there be in a little less pain.

Further Resources

The Care and Keeping of You series by American Girl

Periods Gone Public: Taking a Stand for Menstrual Equity by Jennifer Weiss-Wolf

Nancy's Nook Endometriosis Education, a Facebook.com Group

Center for Endometriosis Care: centerforendo.com

How to Be a Period Activist

- **Read about periods!** You are doing that now! There are some further resources on page 332 if you want to read more.
- **Talk about periods!** Talking about periods is the number one easiest way to help erase period stigma.
- **Donate period products to those in need.** Women's shelters and homeless shelters often need menstrual hygiene products, underwear, and pads. Organize your friends and collect unused period products that you can donate.
- **Make sure the machines in your school are stocked, and talk to someone if they aren't.** Easy access to menstrual products is a luxury many people who get periods do not have.
- **Share your products!** If you have the ability to share unused tampons and pads, you could leave some in the school bathroom or share with a friend in need.
- **Write to your government representative** and tell them we need menstrual equity in all government buildings, including schools and prisons.
- **Use your skills to speak up for those in need!** You are an awesome person with unique skills—use those skills in a creative way to speak up for period equity. Maybe it means organizing a march, making art, writing a song, dancing for charity, or writing a play! There are so many ways that you can uniquely help shatter period stigma in your own pad.

Acknowledgments

This book would not have been possible without the support, skills, and thoughtful input of many people.

To the Williams, Schneemann, and Louie families, thank you for the time, babysitting, traveling, orange tea, and support to help us find our voices and make this book possible; Kaley Bales, for being an amazing colorist and bringing life to our book; Minju Chang and BookStop Literary Agency, who have been a constant source of support and feedback; to Emily Feinberg, a period champion and the backbone of this book; to Jen Besser, Connie Hsu, Kate Jacobs, Mekisha Telfer, Luisa Berguiristain, Megan Abbate, and Tess Weitzner for your editorial feedback and for making sure the book flowed well; Andrew Arnold and Molly Johanson, for taking the art to the next level; Hayley Jozwiak, for detail-oriented feedback; Jill Freshney and Elizabeth Clark, for their expertise; to the entire warehouse team for getting this book into the hands of readers; to every person with a period, may you not have shame and may we break stigma together; and to you, dear reader, for reading our book. You all are bloody awesome!

We dedicate this book to all who have had or will have a period! You are not alone.

—Lily and Karen

Published by First Second
First Second is an imprint of Roaring Brook Press, a division
of Holtzbrinck Publishing Holdings Limited Partnership
120 Broadway, New York, NY 10271

Don't miss your next favorite book from First Second!
For the latest updates go to firstsecondnewsletter.com and sign up for our enewsletter.

Library of Congress Control Number: 2019930666

ISBN (Hardcover): 978-1-250-30572-5
ISBN (Paperback): 978-1-250-14317-4

Our books may be purchased in bulk for promotional, educational, or business use.
Please contact your local bookseller or the Macmillan Corporate and Premium Sales Department
at (800) 221-7945 ext. 5442 or by email at MacmillanSpecialMarkets@macmillan.com.

First edition, 2020
Cover design by Andrew Arnold
Interior book design by Dave Kopka
Color by Kaley Bales, Lily Williams, and Karen Schneemann
Printed in China by 1010 International Limited, North Point, Hong Kong

Penciled with Blackwing pencils. Inked and colored digitally in Photoshop.

10 9 8 7 6 5 4 3 2 1